Tiny Treasures

FICTION FROM MIDDLESEX

First published in Great Britain in 2010 by
Young Writers, Remus House, Coltsfoot Drive,
Peterborough, PE2 9JX
Tel (01733) 890066 Fax (01733) 313524
Website: www.youngwriters.co.uk

Foreword

Since Young Writers was established in 1990, our aim has been to promote and encourage written creativity amongst children and young adults. By giving aspiring young authors the chance to be published, Young Writers effectively nurtures the creative talents of the next generation, allowing their confidence and writing ability to grow.

With our latest fun competition, *The Adventure Starts Here ...*, primary school children nationwide were given the tricky challenge of writing a story with a beginning, middle and an end in just fifty words.

The diverse and imaginative range of entries made the selection process a difficult but enjoyable task with stories chosen on the basis of style, expression, flair and technical skill. A fascinating glimpse into the imaginations of the future, we hope you will agree that this entertaining collection is one that will amuse and inspire the whole family.

Contents

St Mary's Catholic Primary School, Uxbridge

St Mary's RC Primary School, Isleworth

The Mini Sagas

Fire

Once there was a dragon. It was weird, it had two heads. They were called Finney and Pepper. They could not agree with anything, that's why they could not fly or breathe fire. Kylee was a friend of theirs. Pepper heard a scream in the night.

'It's Kylee!' screamed Pepper.

Chloe Dyson (10)
Cowley St Laurence CE Primary School

You'll Never Walk Alone!

Liverpool! The crowd goes wild! It's going to
go to penalties! Who's willing to take a penalty?
Suddenly, Shevchenco's kick could win the match
for AC Milan. If Dudek saves it, Liverpool are
champions of Europe! Jerzy's doing crazy legs; he
saves it! Liverpool! The Kop goes wild! *Again!*

Aaron Kelati (9)
Cowley St Laurence CE Primary School

New Star

My debut for Arsenal, my aim was to score a hat-trick. Cesc Fabregas played it through to me … one touch, *bang!* 'Oh yes, number two!' Another free kick just outside the box. I ran to shoot. *Yes!* My penalty smacked the back of the net. Woo-hoo! Hat-trick!

Joe Lewis (10)
Cowley St Laurence CE Primary School

Hard Landing

I have landed in a jungle and I am fighting in a
Japanese military base. I am all on my own with
no back-up. I am starving, but luckily I get radio
contact with my base. They send in some supplies
by helicopter … I am going to be OK!

Reiss Tuckwell (9)
Cowley St Laurence CE Primary School

4

Blood Of Dead

I was in a field. I was petrified! Then I heard a
bazooka being shot! All five of us charged towards
them and then it went silent … *bang!* A grenade
landed in front of us! I was OK, but my mate was
hurt and the rest … *dead!*

Oliver Gallagher
Cowley St Laurence CE Primary School

Silent Death

It was dark. It was quiet. As Tom and Jim went
into the forest, they heard a strange noise! They
went in further to investigate. A scream … and
they ran. They lost contact and were never seen
again! It was dark. Everything was silent …

George Brookfield
Cowley St Laurence CE Primary School

6

Wow, Scared, Wacky!

Imagine a world where I could fly. *Wow*, I thought
to myself, *it would be incredible!* Suddenly, I
moved. Who was that?

'Anyone there?' I bellowed in a scared voice.

A voice replied, 'Yes, who are you? I'm Mr Blake,
what's wrong?'

'Everything is weird and very wacky,' I whispered.

Danny Gallagher (10)
Cowley St Laurence CE Primary School

7

Lost In The Dark

I'm lost in the dark; I don't know where I am! Do you know where I am? I'm in a dark place, I can't see anybody. I'm frightened, I'm petrified! I can hear a sound, it's coming closer … and closer … and closer. What shall I do? Somebody help me!

Sophie Coole (10)
Cowley St Laurence CE Primary School

It's Only Us

It was Halloween. I opened my one and only present. When I opened it, two zombies came in. I was really petrified! I ran upstairs and hid under my covers. I heard them dashing up the stairs! They pulled the covers off me. They shouted, 'Do you like our costumes?'

Shannon Peterson
Cowley St Laurence CE Primary School

Return Of The Gladiator

It is a hot, sunny day in Rome. Zeus, the greatest
gladiator, is fighting a ferocious lion to protect
his family. The crowd are baying for blood and
cheering with excitement. Zeus spears the
roaring lion! He waves triumphantly to the
crowd, but the lion is not dead ...

O'Neil Duff (10)
Cowley St Laurence CE Primary School

Shark Slayer

Under the deep blue sea was a shark slayer; he
defended his fish city.
One day the most destructive shark came to
destroy the city. Who could save them from the
terrifying shark?
The enemies came face to face. They battled …
to victory. No more sharks here!

Oliver Taylor (10)
Cowley St Laurence CE Primary School

Daring Blood

There was a vampire who lived in a gloomy, terrifying and powerful sea called the Bermuda Triangle, the devil sea! Anyone brave who saw the blood or ever came near would evaporate forever! Some say it's just a trick that teenagers play on people. But who dares to go near?

Luqman Khir (10)
Cowley St Laurence CE Primary School

Out Of Order

I went to the funfair; it was the best ride ever! It
went faster … and faster. Suddenly, it *stopped!*
Everything went quiet. I asked to get off, but
nobody heard. I asked again, they told me to wait
… and *wait!* I shouted, 'Help!' but still nobody
listened. Out of order!

Amira Soliman (10)
Cowley St Laurence CE Primary School

War: A Story With A Twist In The Tale

Two tribes glare at each other across the muddy battleground. Fists waving, flags flying. As the turmoil reaches a crescendo, songs of pride and victory vibrate with every heartbeat. The masses bay for the defeat and doom of their enemies.

The referee's whistle blows and …

The football match begins!

Chloe Wretham (10)

Norbury School

Jennette's Nightmare

Molly and Jennette were at the beach. They were enjoying themselves when a massive wave hit the sand. It was a tsunami. Everyone at the beach, including the girls, ran away screaming. The tsunami was heading their way …

Jennette woke up, relieved. 'Just a dream,' she reassured herself.

Beanica Ryanne Tripoli (9)
Norbury School

The Owl And The Tomcat

Owl said, 'Stay away.'
Tom said, 'Yeah right! That's my kitty!'
Owl dive-bombed Tom, pecked his head.
Tom scratched, brought Owl down, *bang!*
Tom sat on Owl's head. 'You foul creature!'
They tumbled over each other till Owl cried out,
'OK, you win, take the feathered kittens too!'

Mariam Ghuwel (10)
Norbury School

16

Shadow

As Molly turned around, she saw a white shadow.
'What was that?' she asked herself. Well, she was
in a haunted house. *'Whoo!'* moaned a ghost.
Molly turned to the exit, but surprisingly, it wasn't
there. What was she going to do?

Zuzanna Gwozdz (10)
Norbury School

The Haunted House

It was a dark night. The haunted house stood in the distance. Ben was on his way home from school. He was curious to see inside the haunted house. Had he never heard the legend? Whoever dares to step inside the huge, scary house shall turn into stone …

Callum Rogers (10)
Norbury School

Ghost In The Mansion

One thundery night there was a family, Mum,
Dad, Sally and Sam.
That night Sally heard a sound. She went
downstairs and opened the front door. Her
brother was behind her. When he tapped her, she
screamed. Their mum woke up. She whispered,
'There's no ghost, it's just a wolf.'

Damini Chudasama (9)
Norbury School

A Jittery Moment

It was a cold, breezy evening. I was walking home from school, all alone. Suddenly, I was facing a fierce and stout dog obstructing my path. He growled. I was stunned, almost paralysed with fear. Just then, Mum's yell woke me abruptly. 'A nightmare, thank goodness!' I muttered to myself.

Archita Tayal (10)
Norbury School

The Rich, Unknown Bank Robber

There was a man named Jackson Gregstar who
was known as a bank robber.
One day he went and bought some black clothes
and masks with the money he stole last week.
The next day, Jackson was arrested by police for a
bank robbery he'd committed the past week.

Winishan Jesudasan (10)
Norbury School

Baldilocks And The Three Hairs

One joyful day, Baldilocks strolled excitedly
through Egghead village, for that day Sir Hairalot
and his three knights, Care Hair, Bare Hair and
Rare Hair, were coming. Boldilocks rushed
towards them with a few bottles of hair removal
cream.

'Oops! It's everywhere!' shouted Baldilocks.
The knights screamed, 'We're bald!'

Trevin Mabarana (10)
Norbury School

The Magic And The Evil

One night Alfred was cooking with a little help from his magic. Then the door slammed shut. A devil came and he was trying to kill Alfred. They got into a very big fight until the devil found a magic sword and killed Alfred like a cat with tail up.

Antonio Vestiman (10)
Norbury School

My Little Kitten

One summer day, when I came back from school,
I found the kitchen window open and I couldn't
find my cat. I went outside to look for my cat.
I was looking in the park, shops, streets, but I
couldn't find her anywhere.
The next day she came back.

Linas Daugela (9)
Norbury School

24

Alone In The Desert

Ben was all alone in the desert at night, when he saw a gigantic sandstorm. *'Arrgh!'* shouted Ben. He wondered how he'd got himself into this mess. Suddenly, he heard a voice saying, 'Wake up! Wake up!' It was Mum. It was all a dream.

David Davidovic (10)
Norbury School

Something Horrible Happens To Lucy

Lucy was alone for the whole day. It was dark and also raining. Suddenly, the door opened. Lucy was frightened. She tried to hide but she couldn't. Someone came inside and switched on the lights. Then Lucy noticed that it wasn't a ghost - it was her parents!

Margi Patel (10)
Norbury School

The Little Pig And The Evil Bell

One day one pig decided to make his own house.
Then he saw a girl walking. He said, 'What's your
name?'
She replied, 'Bell.'
'Come to my house.'
'Thanks.'
Then she killed him when they got into the house
and then made him into a leather coat!

Jenika Chudasama (9)
Norbury School

27

Holiday Adventures

Kelly and Bobby Thomson were on their way back from Pontins. But before long the road came to an end. They found themselves in a water wonderland and had lots of fun. After they finished, they went home and went to bed and fell asleep.

Emma Prior (10)
Norbury School

Upset King

Once upon a time, there was a king named DT.
He loved his PSP and book!
One day they went missing. He looked
everywhere but he could not find them, so he
called his best friend who came over. Then his
friend found them. This made DT very happy.

Dionte Bent (10)
Norbury School

Is There A God?

Long ago there was a small boy called Pralad who
believed in God. His dad didn't like this and tried
to stop him from preaching, but Pralad didn't
stop. In the end his dad tried to burn him alive,
but Pralad still survived. This proved there is a
god.

Ashish Sodha (10)
Norbury School

Historical Event

Archimedes was born in Syracuse, the establishment in Sicily. He studied in Alexandria, Egypt. There he studied with the disciples of Euclid and spent the rest of his life in Syracuse. Archimedes defined the principle of the lever and invented the compound pulley.

Haroon Qureshi (10)
Norbury School

Ghostly Goings-On

A girl was very happy. It was her birthday party.
When she went to sleep on that cold night, a
ghost called Holly tried to kill her, but she had an
energy protector to keep her safe, so the little girl
is still alive, even today.

Hayley Gueth-Scott (10)
Norbury School

Mysteries Invade My Soul

Panic was alerted. The atmosphere was as pale as death. My petrified emotions stung my flesh. Anxious, I didn't move an inch. Nervousness bolted through my veins as I trembled all over. I stood - isolated. Misery shook the organs inside me. Where was I? Who was I? What was I?

Reenal Pankhania (11)
North Primary School

The Lost World

The corridor was dark and full of cobwebs when John and Jessy walked through. *What is this?* they wondered. The floor creaked as they walked. Suddenly, a group of bats flew above them. Jessy screamed! John opened a door and they were back home.

'Where were you?' Mum asked.

Dhruvin Vijal Valgi (8)
North Primary School

Shock

Silence and darkness filled the air. She shivered and let out a chilling cry. Another was on the way when she heard *the* creak. She froze with shock. Without warning, everything turned bright. Mum passed biscuits, she nibbled. She waited patiently for the movie to start again, with *the* smile.

Mehak Chandel (9)
North Primary School

Bombs Of Misery!

It was another day, again of misery. Bombs of
sadness were exploding above my head! Again,
a bully walked on top of my heart. Drums
of sadness beat my heart. Life was just a bin!
Butterflies of anguish invaded my body! I was in
shock! I was extremely worried ...

Gurvinder Uppal (10)
North Primary School

Home Alone!

One day I arrived home from school. No one was home and suddenly, I saw a ghost! I was really scared. I screamed and shouted, but it was no use because no one could hear me. A few minutes later, I thought I heard my mum coming, but it was ...

Aleeza Chohan (10)
North Primary School

Alien?

A boy called Joe was coming back from school
and he saw a light. The earth shook. *'Argh!'*
He got home and told his dad and mum. He went
outside to play and saw this blue thing. It told him
it needed to get home. Joe helped it home.

Jasneet Minhas (10)
North Primary School

Who's There?

Louise was at home waiting for her parents.
'They should be back by now,' she murmured.
There was a sudden noise from upstairs. The
squeaking made Louise unsettled. She went
upstairs to investigate. As she approached the top
of the stairs, she saw some boxes …
'Puppies!' she shouted very happily.

Kourtnie Atkinson (10)
Oakington Manor Primary School

Shocking Surprise!

Emily walked through her front door. The house was covered in darkness. She could hear a voice coming from the kitchen. She jumped back and fell on the floor. Emily stood up again, then silently tiptoed on the old, wooden floor that screeched as Emily was heading towards the kitchen …

Shernelle Hickson (11)
Oakington Manor Primary School

Fear

As Sally walked furiously down the extremely cold stairs, the fear of facing her foe engulfed her. She selected her weapon of choice - the great mechanism of sound. There she stood face to face with the grey beast … locked in battle only by sight.
Atchoo! Grumpily, she began to vacuum.

Rhys Urssher (11)
Oakington Manor Primary School

The Killer Griffin

A demon shaped like a griffin dug its lethal claws into a dragon's eye. Then it released flesh-eating worms to devour the dragon! It was now one step closer to finding the demon antidote. It was hidden in the demon's dungeon. Therefore it could morph into a human again.

Prakul Patel (11)
Oakington Manor Primary School

42

Monsters?

The room is as dark as a cave. An unpleasant scent pollutes the air. My fingertips begin to get numb. I search for the light switch as quickly as I can. *Monsters!* Thousands of them surround me. Oh, wait! I am in a mirror house. The monster is … *me!* Whoops!

Rianna Nurse (10)
Oakington Manor Primary School

A Hamster's Escape

Jodie was alone in the flat with only her hamster for comfort. It sat in its cage gawking at her until it was fed. Grabbing it from its cage, she flopped it in its blue ball. When Jodie left the room, it knocked the ball onto the wall and escaped …

Taylor Cumberbatch (11)
Oakington Manor Primary School

The Birthday Mystery!

Tick-tock! It was 8 o'clock. Everyone was up
early to wrap Rianna's present.
Ding-dong! Rianna unlocked the door. In a wink
of an eye she was snatched by a masked man!
Why was she taken? The door opened. 'Boo!'
everyone shouted. 'Surprise! Happy birthday!'
The mystery was solved!

Paris Harding (10)
Oakington Manor Primary School

The Smile From Mrs Notay

The children fell silent as Mrs Notay walked
through. Her eyes told a terrible story. Something
was wrong, but she never said nor did she smile.
Lucy was new and full of happiness. She ran into
the room and screamed, 'Good morning.'
Mrs Notay stood shocked and weirdly just smiled!

Pariise-Jade David-McLeod (11)
Oakington Manor Primary School

Eve's Scary Shock

It was an ordinary evening. Eve was relaxing on her cosy couch. Suddenly, she heard a creak behind her. She turned around to see who or what it was …

'Argh!' she screamed in shock.
'Boo!' her brothers shouted.

Bria Fontenelle (11)
Oakington Manor Primary School

In A Strop

Bang! the door went as Keddy slammed it in a
strop. He was frustrated with his father, so he
decided to walk to his mum's house. Walking
down the street, he realised what danger he had
got himself into. Just then his dad picked him up.
Everything was OK!

Freddie Lawley-Wakelin (11)
Oakington Manor Primary School

The Creepy Cottage

'Sam, I dare you to enter the cottage in the forest.'
'I was planning to anyway!' Sam replied.
After school, Sam ventured through the frightening, dark forest leading to the creepy cottage. He looked into the window and noticed a flickering light. He saw something petrifying.
'OK, I'm going now!'

Serenmyst Scott (11)
Oakington Manor Primary School

The Fall Of The Mighty Dragon

The flares of the fierce dragon transformed the cities of Bell-Frontier into ash. Two teenagers were the last survivors. As they tried to escape, quick shivers ran down their spines. A screech was a sign that something had slaughtered the foul beast.

Dhruv Gajjar (11)
Oakington Manor Primary School

Alone

As the night slowly crept into the sky, Kylie was alone in an abandoned house. The floorboard creaked. The window was open, letting in a cool breeze, the curtains flapping free. Somehow, Kylie felt like someone else was in the house. Suddenly the door handle turned, she was right!

Leah Hardy-Deacon (11)
Oakington Manor Primary School

Haunted House

Scared and horrified, I slowly inched like a slug
into the ghostly haunted house. My eyes were my
hands, my jaw hung down. A terrifying creature
with blood dripping down, its feet coming
towards me, one by one. 'Argh!' I yelled to my
death. I finally saw it …

Aisha Nadim (10)
Oakington Manor Primary School

Surprise

Chris was rushing home, late for a family
gathering. He threw open the front door.
Surprisingly, the lights were off. He heard
something in the room. Grabbing the baseball bat,
he turned on the lights ...
'Surprise!' they exclaimed. 'Happy birthday!'
His reaction was ecstatic.

Vaidik Pindolia (11)
Oakington Manor Primary School

Another Addition

As I turned the key in the door on my return from school, I heard my mother scream. I rushed upstairs frantically in a panic, wondering what was happening. The room was heaving with people. I looked at Dad crying. 'You have a beautiful baby sister!' he said with excitement.

John Seraphin-Whyte (11)
Oakington Manor Primary School

54

Alone

A girl named Jessica was at home alone. Her mum and dad went to work. *Ding-dong* went the door. Jessica opened it. There was nothing there, so she shut the door. *Ding-dong* went the door again. This time there was nothing except a letter. She opened it …

Sabiha Rahman (8)
Oakington Manor Primary School

Princess The Horse!

As Vicki was riding her horse, Princess, Jessica was planning a surprise. When Vicki came back there was a party because it was Princess' birthday. Jessica bought Princess a horse rug and a pink lead rope. Everyone else bought a mint or apples.

Bipashna Mukhia (9)
Oakington Manor Primary School

Chocolate Girl

One day there was a beautiful girl named Elly. She loved to eat chocolate. Elly ate so much chocolate that she got fat. She was rolling around and she scared her cousin and her mother. Suddenly, she exploded and she was never seen or heard of again!

Hasiba Husseini (9)
Oakington Manor Primary School

Magic

'Come on, we are going to be late,' moaned Lucy
to Mary.
Mary walked down the hall. However, it was not
a hall, it was a cave. In the cave was a golden box.
She opened it slowly and it cried, terrified. 'Please
help me and look after me well!'

Adiba Husseini (11)
Oakington Manor Primary School

Ghostly Silence

Silence. I was just about to fall asleep when I
heard the door shut. My parents were asleep.
Who could it be? I was frightened. I didn't dare
move. There was silence again. I heard footsteps
coming upstairs. It whispered my name! I
switched my lamp on ...
My brother!

Muskaan Vekereya (9)
Oakington Manor Primary School

Fairy Fight-Off

Melana was on holiday with her family in Florida. Melana wanted to be an explorer when she grew up.

As she was walking, she buckled on *air!* Suddenly, she was pulled down a tunnel! A *fairy* told her that she seriously needed help. That was the beginning of Melana's adventure ...

Antonia-Jade Luke (10)
Oakington Manor Primary School

Dare

There were children playing on the footpath, named Jack, Joe and Robert. It was Robert's birthday so his friends dared him to walk into a spooky house. Robert went inside. He felt frightened. Now the room was so cold.
'Surprise!'
'Wow, this is the best surprise party I have had!'

Dilan Hirani (9)
Oakington Manor Primary School

Lost And Lonely

Janine woke up and as usual she swiftly ran down the stairs to greet her parents. However, it was awfully quiet in the house and no one was there. She searched her street, but no one, no one at all could be seen. Janine prayed fearfully this was a dream …

Amal Ahmed (9)
Oakington Manor Primary School

Close To Death

Emma glanced out of the aeroplane's window, until she recognised that the plane was gradually tilting downwards. Emma immediately established that the plane was not landing, it was crash-landing! Everybody was gasping for help! Just when the plane was about to collide, Emma woke up …

'Ahhh! That was close!'

Besheer Al-Khayat (10)
Oakington Manor Primary School

The Life Of Emma Hardson

It was the first day of spring. Emma Hardson was preparing to go to school. It was the best private school in Liverpool. Her father was in Italy with his business. He promised to go back today for her birthday party. Emma was excited. She invited her friends and Edward.

Olivia Mauer (10)
Oakington Manor Primary School

At School Alone!

The school was all empty except for Zahrah, the kind one and Marcus, the bully. Everyone liked Zahrah. Everyone hated Marcus. Suddenly, Marcus jumped in front of Zahrah and took her bag full of valuables and her beautiful coat. Then, after he chased her, she called the police.

Alice Muratovic (10)
Oakington Manor Primary School

Opposite Day!

In the playground, Lola was talking to some rude girls. They said it was 'opposite day'. So Lola was saying that Janet, her best friend, smelled and was ugly, fat and rude. Janet walked by. They started arguing. Lola tried to explain. Finally, Janet believed Lola and they stayed friends.

Kyra-Marie Smith (9)
Oakington Manor Primary School

A Holiday Adventure

Tom and Jill were on the beach. They decided to walk around it. They got lost for two hours. After two hours of exploring where they were, they found their way back to the beach. Their parents were really worried about them and gave them an enormous, loving, caring hug!

Micah Phillips-Davis (10)
Oakington Manor Primary School

Females Not Allowed!

Whilst digging the garden, Lily discovered an old coin. She polished it and began to tingle. Suddenly, she found herself transported to the Ancient Greek Olympics. Females weren't allowed! 'Hey you!' a man in a toga yelled. Frightened, Lily ran. She rubbed the coin and whooshed back to 2010. Phew!

Emily Walmsley-Smith (10)
Oakington Manor Primary School

The Ghosts Of Lightning Street

One stormy night, the ghosts of Lightning Street
lurked in the shadows, floating down from a roof.
A spine-tingling scream was echoing. The ghosts
had claimed another victim!
Jake, eleven, was determined to find his friend,
but in the final battle, Jake was sadly turned into a
ghost himself!

Abhinav Vudathu (10)
Oakington Manor Primary School

Friends Once More

One day, the fairies, Poppy and Rosie, were
having an argument. Poppy wanted to go to the
theatre and Rosie to the museum. While they
were fighting, both the theatre and museum
closed. They soon realised that and apologised
to each other. Later, they vowed never to argue
ever again.

Nisha Moktan (10)
Oakington Manor Primary School

70

Wanna Replay It?

I was at the market when I saw someone familiar
crossing the road. It was the bully! Phew! He
went round the corner, nowhere near me.
Silence, until something unexpectedly moved. A
black figure was passing by. Suddenly, there was
an almighty scream! My only weapon was my
pen ...

Roua Oubira (9)
Oakington Manor Primary School

Fun-Hating Teacher Strikes Again!

Sally called Miss Iwo's name. 'Can we do something fun?'
Miss Iwo was furious. She screeched, *'No!* Sally, you know I absolutely hate fun! In the box.'
'But Miss, I'm scared of the box.'
'I don't care. Class, stop laughing immediately or you'll all be in the box.'
'Yes, Miss.'

Teya Powell (10)
Oakington Manor Primary School

72

The Great Win!

I arrived at football, late. I thought I would be sub.
As I got closer, Kevin shouted, 'We're one short.'
I ran straight on and passed to Nico who scored
the first of two goals. We had done it, we had
won our first match and I was not sub.

Alfie Langan (9)
Oakington Manor Primary School

The Petrified, Unexpected Surprise

Stella entered her friend's haunted house. The ghostly eyes appeared and there was a sudden bang! She was petrified but still waited for her friend. A hand tapped Stella on her back.

'Argh!'

'Happy friends' anniversary.'

Stella didn't see that coming! They gave each other a warm cuddle of joy.

Pooja Thakore (9)

Oakington Manor Primary School

Ghosts At Home!

Jack was alone at home. It was dark outside. He was watching TV in his room when the door closed. Suddenly, he saw something move under the door. he slowly walked towards the door and opened it. He saw a shadow moving around the corner and began to follow it ...

Umi Patel (10)
Oakington Manor Primary School

75

Petrified Boy

Joe came to a rusty, haunted house. Just as he went in, the floor started to crack and smash into pieces. He silently walked upstairs. Suddenly, a ghost tapped him on the back! To his shock, it was only his sister who tapped him. Relieved, Joe ambled home.

Zaynab Agoro (10)
Oakington Manor Primary School

The End?

I set out for my journey. I planned to explore all the diversity of America. Once on board the plane, a ghostly figure shot my mum and took over the plane. I called the cops. No answer. I jumped off …
'Argh!' Thud! I lay unconscious.

Dion Maingi (10)
Oakington Manor Primary School

Untitled

After an extended amount of time, Lucy arrived there. She had the sacred, golden ring which had been lost for years. This ring was created long before her ancestors existed. It had great powers and responsibility. Still, she had the ring.

Ilhan Dirshe (10)
Oakington Manor Primary School

78

Voices In The Air

In that very moment, Rosie heard someone's
voice calling, 'Rosie, Rosie dear.'
Rosie quickly ran to the person who was calling
her. It was her dad. She was very happy and she
gave her dad a big hug.

Zoreen Haidri (9)
Oakington Manor Primary School

Moving Houses

Yesterday Tom was moving house. He was so sad
that he had to move house. He said that he was
going to miss his friend, Biff. But when he moved
house, his mum told him, 'Biff can still come to
your house.'
After that Tom was very happy.

Rim Baajour (9)
Oakington Manor Primary School

Disappeared

Polly was walking in the woods, collecting berries
for jam-making, but there were no berries. Then
she saw them up in the tree, so she climbed up
to get them. In doing this, she absentmindedly
knocked a ghost. The berries vanished at that
moment without her touching them.

Kulsum Gulamhusein (9)
St Helen's School, Northwood

The Not Ugly Duckling

In a gorgeous yellow field lived an ugly duckling
and his family.
'You're ugly,' they would tease him.
One morning they were so rude to him, he ran
away to Farmer's Cottage. Really, he was not
ugly. When he saw himself in the pond, the others
were the ugly ones.

Tania Dandachli (9)
St Helen's School, Northwood

The Speaking Rabbit

'Waaaa!' said Charlotte.
'Don't cry,' said a mysterious voice.
'I can't control it,' sobbed Charlotte. 'Wait, who
was that?'
'Me,' said the chirpy rabbit.
'No, no, that can't be.' But he was talking so it
had to be true. She stared in amazement. 'I've
never seen a talking rabbit.'

Hannah Bonning (9)
St Helen's School, Northwood

The Vampire And Me!

'Ow!'
I heard a scream. I glanced at the boy soaked in blood, shaking in fear. I walked closer and saw a red-eyed vampire glaring at me. He came closer and closer as I stepped further and further back. I reached in my pocket and screamed at my blood ...

Safiya Merali (10)
St Helen's School, Northwood

A Crack In The Ice

Her scream bounced off the pond's icy surface.
Frozen claws scraped her leg where the ice caved
in. Was this it? She had wanted more than 15
years of life. As her head bobbed under there was
a complete blackout.
A girl lay on a hospital bed. Her heartbeat,
stopped.

Lydia Wareing (11)
St Helen's School, Northwood

A Monstrous Roar

Henry entered the dark corridor. The school
was quiet at night. Suddenly, he heard a noise.
A monstrous roar filled the hall. Henry's heart
skipped a beat as a giant beast turned the corner.
The beast eyed Henry up and down, then
charged. The next minute the hall was empty.

Alison Brody (11)
St Helen's School, Northwood

The Matchstick

Jack crept into the deep wood. His mouth trembled in the moonlight. He struck a match, shaking, and held it up. The match blew out. Suddenly, a grumbling noise echoed loudly. He pleadingly fell to the ground when screams filled the misty air. A towering shadow crept away …

Harriet Pitcher (10)
St Helen's School, Northwood

The Closet

Sarah was going out with her friends. She looked
for the best dress she had. As soon as she found
the perfect dress, she fell inside her closet and
the closet fell out of the window. Sarah lay on
the ground, dead. Her mum screamed when she
heard a bang!

Patricia Odysseos Suther (11)
St Helen's School, Northwood

Roof Adventure

'Silky, come down from there. You know you
want to.'
My cat, Silky, was stuck on the roof. I was as well.
Silky jumped down onto the stone patio. The roof
was starting to crumble. 'Help!' I edged away.
Silky's miaow echoed around the garden. The
roof fell. *Crunch.* *'Ouch!'*

Sophie Gottlieb (10)
St Helen's School, Northwood

Where's Rover?

Phoebe was in bed. Rover kept barking. She
suddenly woke. 'Rover!' she yelled and went to
see what was making her dog upset. He couldn't
be found. Phoebe went back to bed.
When she turned the shower on the next
morning, blood and fur splattered all over the
bath tub …

Olivia Booth (11)
St Helen's School, Northwood

The Dripping Tap

Kate was at home alone. She heard someone
parking outside. A door slammed. Someone
knocked at the door. Stupidly, she answered the
door. He told her he was a plumber.
When her parents got home, they couldn't find
her. They turned on the tap. Blood dripped
out ...

Poppy Tracey (10)
St Helen's School, Northwood

The Scream

At 4am I woke up hearing a scream at Katie's house. We rushed downstairs to the basement. I punched the air hearing a thump as I got tackled in the dark. The light turned on. Katie lay there dead. What had I done?

Tanya Kanani (11)
St Helen's School, Northwood

The Car From Nowhere

Ben was lost in the middle of a murky wood,
the trees were towering over him. Wolves
howled and came closer like uncontrollable cats.
The wolves seemed to look at him deliciously.
Suddenly, a car rampaged between the trees.
The wolves were gone. Where had the car come
from?

Maitri Pindolia (11)
St Helen's School, Northwood

Lost In The Dark Forest

'Tigger,' murmured Pooh. Pooh was all alone in a dark forest, trembling in the moonlight.
Suddenly, there was a crack. 'Is that you, Tigger?' Pooh screamed and ran around. 'Tigger said he would be here,' shouted Pooh angrily.
'Boo! Happy birthday,' screamed Tigger.
'Oh, thank you!' laughed Pooh, jumping excitedly.

Mallaika Virani (11)
St Helen's School, Northwood

94

A Death Dream

She twitched and turned. Her unknown twin,
bloody hands, held her heart up in the air,
triumphant, herself, dead on the ground. Dr Finn
found her. I watched from below, the Devil by my
side. I, the twin, will reach your dreams one day
and decide your fate. I'm *Death!*

Ria Gupta (10)
St Helen's School, Northwood

The Lost Girl

One hot, sunny day, Tom and Sarah were playing
in the garden. Tom said, 'I'm going to get a drink.'
When he came back, Sarah was not there.
Then he remembered the fatal car crash three
devastating years ago …

Talia Godfrey (11)
St Helen's School, Northwood

Flat 21

It was midnight. In flat 21 something was following me, up close, breathing on my neck. I turned around but couldn't see anything. It was dark. I ran out of the haunted flat. It was still there! My heart stopped. It was white and floating.

'I've been waiting … '

Risha Amin (11)
St Helen's School, Northwood

Knock, Knock

Knock, knock, knock. There it is again. It's been haunting me for years. I'm going to investigate once and for all today!

I creep cautiously towards the frightful noise. It's getting louder …

'*Argh!* Something's grabbed me! Somebody save me! Father, Fatheeeeer … '

Ah, it's morning. That was a very odd dream!

Tegan Drew (9)
St Helen's School, Northwood

Up, Up And Away!

Me and my family decided to go to the park. My
younger brother loved the curvy slides. He said,
'It is like a Smartie tube, round, round and round.'
I rushed to the swings. I went so high that I
whooshed over. I became invisible. I went to
another world …

Natasha Dixon (10)
St Helen's School, Northwood

Humpty-Dumpty's Paint Problem

It was a breezy, sunny day. Humpty-Dumpty,
the egg, sat on his wall. He grew eggs near his
wall and decided to give them an Easter effect.
Humpty-Dumpty held a big bucket of paint over
the eggs, when *splat!* The paint went right on his
head. 'Oh bother!'

Celia Dipple (10)
St Helen's School, Northwood

Going To The Zoo

Sally was telling her dad that she was going to the
zoo.
Later, when she drove to the zoo, she suddenly
remembered that she was scared of monkeys.
When she got to the zoo and saw the monkeys,
she leapt into a stranger's arms, then ran away
screaming!

Beth Lewis (9)
St Helen's School, Northwood

Groovy Greek Heroes

'Grab your swords, tie up your shoes, it's time for the battle of dance. Hip, hop, glide, cling, clash, closh, let's get dancing, spinning off stage only to hop right back on. Glide in the light and swing your hips. It's the battle of dance!'

Jessica Garner-Patel (9)
St Helen's School, Northwood

Planing

'Shhh,' said Mum to Sammy when they were on the plane.

Sammy would not be quiet as it was noisy and he couldn't hear. He'd been listening hard to the music and not to his mum talking.

A couple of hours later the plane had a sudden crash …

Tulsi Popat (9)
St Helen's School, Northwood

Start, Camera, Action

Suddenly, I heard an eerie echo. I gingerly thought to myself, *where is it coming from?* I felt inquisitive in mind, so I took further steps. I found a damp, murky hole so I crept until I reached the summit. However, I saw a real ghost. Suddenly - 'Camera, action!'

Olivia Millet (9)
St Helen's School, Northwood

The Easter Bunny

One bright, sunny day there was a bunny, he
adored Easter eggs.
One day Floppy ate a magic Easter egg. He
turned into an Easter bunny. He grew big boinging
feet and big floppy ears and now he delivers
Easter eggs to everyone in the town. I love
Floppy.

Maya Taylor (7)
St Helen's School, Northwood

The Easter Bunny

Walking in the woods, I spied the injured Easter
bunny. Beside him was a basket of patterned eggs.
Oh dear, the bunny had a tear trickling down
his cheek. I kissed him gently. A flash of light
appeared. Four red robins flew the egg basket
over the world delivering eggs.

Hannah Wood (8)
St Helen's School, Northwood

The Easter Egg Hunt

Once upon a time there was a girl called Tilly and her best friend called Milly. They both had golden brown hair and emerald-green eyes.
On a fine Easter day, when Milly was at Tilly's house, Tilly's mum had hidden some chocolate bunnies, they found them all!

Yemisi Onigbanjo (10)
St Helen's School, Northwood

The Hungry Baby Bird

Sniffy was hungry. His mother was out hunting
but she hadn't returned and he was worried. He
was getting restless, he opened his tiny beak and
chirped quietly. Sniffy was a small baby barn owl
with silky feathers and shining eyes. Suddenly,
Mother Owl arrived home. He nuzzled into her.

Sabina Ford (10)
St Helen's School, Northwood

Little Mr Muffet And The Ghost

A small boy came home from school. The coach dropped him off. He went inside and called, 'Mum? Dad?' Nobody answered. He went to the toilet. He sat down. Suddenly, a ghost came and sat beside him. It laughed evilly, showing his blood-dripping fangs … the boy ate him savagely!

Alice Berman (10)
St Helen's School, Northwood

The Discovery

Oooh! Katie was having a picnic when something sparkly attracted her attention, it was a beautiful pearl necklace. She quickly picked it up and looked at it carefully. 'Wow! what a pretty necklace, it will go nicely with my white skirt and blouse. I shall take it home to Mother.'

Jessica Wainwright (10)
St Helen's School, Northwood

The Terrible Flight!

One day, Sue and her family were at the airport
ready for a holiday. 'I'm hungry.' Sue said, so they
went to a restaurant. As they ate, gate Nineteen
closed.

'Oh no! We have missed our flight!' said Mum. So
they didn't have a relaxing, fun holiday after all.

Mya Patel (10)
St Helen's School, Northwood

Humpty Red Riding Hood

Humpty Dumpty sat on a wall. He was extremely bored. He phoned his friend Little Red Riding Hood. She came over very quickly to help Humpty with his spellings. Suddenly there was a *thump* and the sound of hooves galloping. Little Red went home with all the king's men sobbing.

Hannah Speller (9)
St Helen's School, Northwood

112

Beth And The Bakers

Beth skipped to the bakers to get a magnificent cake for her and her baby brother. She requested a cake as blue as the sea with icing like a golden crown. She said that the cake must be patted, pricked, marked with B and cooked to perfection!

Annabelle Lee (9)
St Helen's School, Northwood

The Zooming Bear

A zooming teddy bear came into the garden and
jumped into the pool and said,
'Round and round the splashes like a colourful
whale,
one spin, two spin and a huge splash to knock you
over!'
He got out of the pool and dried himself off with
a huge towel.

Imogene Munns (10)
St Helen's School, Northwood

The Ghostly Fright

One stormy night, Elizabeth came home from
school, there was something strange going on.
With the wonky stairs, Elizabeth heard several
noises. She galloped towards the creepy kitchen.
The vase changed, the clock struck midnight,
moon shimmering. 'It's over!' Lying, shrieking on
the floor. 'Oh, it's my cat!' Laughing.

Ella Patel (10)
St Helen's School, Northwood

Horse Flying High

I was rocking on my rocking horse. Suddenly
it started to sprout wings, I wanted to scream.
Then it flew out of my window, up, up into the
sky. We flew past the clouds, over a rainbow, past
the Eiffel Tower.
I screamed, woke up and fell out of bed!

Emma Van Hentenryck (8)
St Helen's School, Northwood

The Magic Unicorn

The moor was dark and I rustled through the long, yellow grass. Suddenly I heard something galloping. I was hurled up onto an enchanted multi-coloured unicorn! As I floated high, the unicorn presented me a necklace, but threw me onto a delicate cloud, where I stayed.

'Wakey, wakey,' called Mum.

Rani Mandalia (7)
St Helen's School, Northwood

Panda Days

There was once a panda that ate all day and
didn't stop until midnight. All her friends shouted,
'You eat too much!' So she ate more and more
bamboo. She was so angry she stomped and as
she stomped, she heard a bubbling noise and she
popped like a firework!

Tiffany Wong (8)
St Helen's School, Northwood

118

My Holiday

I went to the seaside with my friend and we found a bottle. Out popped a sapphire genie. I wished to travel on a roller coaster. My friend wished to try the funfair. I felt sick. The funfair was closed. I woke up, it was a dream!

Anna Rowan (8)
St Helen's School, Northwood

Easter Bunnies In Mexico

I came out of my house in Mexico. I stared into
the sparkly water and there I found an Easter
water bunny. I was amazed! I tried to touch it. I
couldn't! I stared into the red sun. Another bunny!
Then it started to fade away. It was Easter!

Simi Shah (8)
St Helen's School, Northwood

Zeus' Problem That Was Not Solved

Zoom, Zeus' lightning bolt struck Perseus, god of the sea, in the face. Zeus sent Hermes to deliver a message to Perseus, saying sorry. *Bang!* A clash of thunder hit Hermes, knocking him unconscious. Perseus didn't receive any message. Hermes landed on a rough, juicy olive tree. Zeus went mad!

Orla Forsyth (8)
St Helen's School, Northwood

The Titchy Mouse

In the little hut, on the beach, there was a creak and almighty bang! I didn't feel I was safe. I decided to switch on the huge lights. When I looked, it was a titchy mouse on the creaky floorboard. I was glad I was safe from that little mouse!

Neha Beri (8)
St Helen's School, Northwood

The Ginger Shoe

'Food, I need food,' woofed the magical puppy. Suddenly he spotted the ginger shoe. 'Woof, woof,' he barked, cheering with delight. Just then the door flew open and a fat lady walked in. 'How cute,' she said, as she noticed the magical puppy chewing the large, wide, ginger shoe.

Alisha Moloo (7)
St Helen's School, Northwood

Timmy Adopted A Kitten

Timmy walked towards the tangled rubbish bin. As he approached it, something moved! Picking through the rubbish, he discovered an injured kitten trying to escape. Timmy gently lifted the limping kitten from the tangled mess. 'There, there kitty.' Timmy snuggled the tiny animal into his coat pocket and walked home.

Sarah Andraous (8)

St Helen's School, Northwood

124

A Troubled Horse

One day I noticed a troubled horse and every time he jumped I realised he couldn't speak. From that day on he couldn't 'neigh'. I helped the poor horse get his sound back by practising and practising, and after much hard work he was free to 'neigh' again.

Rianna Modi (7)
St Helen's School, Northwood

The Mysterious Voice

Martha was upstairs studying. She decided to get a drink. The house seemed deserted as Martha crept downstairs. Suddenly, a ghostly voice called out, 'Come with me!' Martha was being lifted into the air. She screamed and kicked and nobody would let her go. She looked up. It was Dad!

Kate Hunter (8)
St Helen's School, Northwood

Birthday Girl

This morning a little girl woke up, it was her birthday. She went into her parents' room, they were not there. She was very upset. So she went downstairs and opened the kitchen door and her parents jumped out and said, 'Happy birthday! Did we surprise you sweetheart?'

Katie Martin (8)
St Helen's School, Northwood

Dead People

Cold as ice, deadly as Dracula in the graveyard.
People are sad holding hankies. Passing away
spirits are floating up, people are sobbing, they
never give up. Dusty headstones with bodies
underneath. The sky, dull and ready to rain and
storm. All people in black, heart stops beating.
Dead.

Athena Odysseos Suther (7)
St Helen's School, Northwood

128

Jack And The Ice Cream Drama

Jack licked his ice cream, but suddenly dropped it.
'Oh no!' he exclaimed. The ice cream lady saw his
sad face and felt sorry for him. The ice cream lady
gave Jack an ice cream for five pence and Jack was
very happy. 'Thank you,' he said and smiled.

Ruth Shaw (7)
St Helen's School, Northwood

The Dark Room

Katie was tired, she was very tired. Her room
was dark, it was cold. Suddenly, she heard a trip
then a trap. She went to investigate. She looked
under the bed and nobody was there. She looked
behind the curtains ... there was her fluffy brown
dog behind the curtains!

Yasmin Gulamhusein (7)
St Helen's School, Northwood

130

Terrified Tim

Tim looked out of the window gloomily. He felt a sudden breeze prickle his neck. He wasn't sure where he was but he thought it might just be the wind. He heard a slight creak from the door. He was hoping it was the police, but it wasn't them …

Anika Kaul (7)
St Helen's School, Northwood

The Hair Cutters

The little boy woke up in bed and noticed that his hair was crazy. He told his mum and asked if he could go to the hair cutters. She said yes. So they went to the hair cutters and the hair cutters put magic in and it turned back.

Sorcha Chan (8)
St Helen's School, Northwood

132

The Magical Dog

The dog was lying down on the bed when
something magical happened. The dog fell down
a hole and hurt his head. The dog was on a huge
magical island. He saw lots of strange animals. He
saw a hole and fell down again and was home at
last.

Anouska Chatrath (8)
St Helen's School, Northwood

Mystery Picture

In a dirty, old house there lived a grey old man.
He had … a mystery picture. One day the old
mystery picture vanished.
'Vanished! Vanished!' screamed the old man. 'Oh
no, the picture has gone, it has *gone!*' he cried.
'It's the mystery picture actually,' said his servant.
'Shut up!'

Nikki Forth (8)
St Helen's School, Northwood

134

The Scary Night

John went outside and felt a funny smell. He walked all the way to the pond. He sat down and threw the end of his fishing rod into the water. Then he heard something rustling against the bush. Then he heard someone whistling, 'Boo!'
'Argh!'
'Ha, ha!'

Shriya Thakkar (8)
St Helen's School, Northwood

Magic Robbery

Lucy got out her magic box but her magic was gone! She called the police, they said they were on it. They called their best person for it. Just then the police heard a peculiar voice come out of the phone saying, 'It was me!' The police shivered with fright.

Leah Datta (8)

St Helen's School, Northwood

136

Ghost!

Sally wandered around the graveyard aimlessly.
A shiver ran down her spine. She looked around
and caught sight of a wandering shadow. Sally
followed the mysterious figure until it stopped.
He turned around and introduced himself as
David Bangton, the friendly king. They became
friends. Whenever Sally came, they played.

Beatrice Cox O'Brien (10)
St Helen's School, Northwood

The Single Rose

Sasha stood, deserted, in her very own garden, and she saw a single rose growing from the floral borders. She looked at the rose and saw a small crystal droplet, trickling from the middle. She picked it solemnly. She heard thunder strike and a voice echoed, 'Death.' The world died.

Shivani Shah (10)
St Helen's School, Northwood

Happy Halloween

One windy night a friend came and said, 'Happy Halloween. I was wondering if I could stay for a sleepover?'

'Sure,' I said. 'Let's watch some movies.' Suddenly, a character screamed, 'Boo!' We both screamed, 'Argh!' We were so scared, my friend fainted.

Faaliha Jivraj (8)
St Helen's School, Northwood

Umbrella

One day Umbrella was sleeping when a big,
enormous bang woke her. 'Happy birthday!' said
her stepmother.
'Oh you remembered,' said Umbrella joyfully.
'Oh sorry,' said her stepmother. 'I got it wrong.'
'Oh,' said Umbrella. She started her cleaning in
the dining room.
'Surprise!' shouted everyone.
'Happy birthday!'

Lucy Lipfriend (9)
St Helen's School, Northwood

140

Trick Or Treat?

There was once a haunted house! An old man
lived there. He was very nice but everyone hated
him. A boy knocked on his door and said, 'Trick
or treat?'
The man went into the kitchen, got some sweets
and the boy said, 'Is that you Grandpa?'
'Yes it is.'

Annabel Turner (8)
St Helen's School, Northwood

My Imagination

I crept inside the scary house. I didn't know whose house it was. 'Mum!' I shouted, I was sure I'd heard something. Then I heard footsteps. After I opened the door and ran, I heard a rustle. Out came a cute little cat. My imagination!

Beth Cook (9)
St Helen's School, Northwood

What Happened Next?

Lily and James decided to take the next road down. This was the street everyone was talking about. They took five steps down and landed in front of something that looked like a haunted house. They set foot into the house. They were greeted by zombies! 'Argh!'

Keya Pindolia (9)
St Helen's School, Northwood

A Mysterious Sound

I was all alone in a little cottage on Raven Road. I stared out of the little cottage window. I gazed at the moon and heard a mysterious sound. I looked around, the sound couldn't be heard. I heard the sound again, then I realised it was my cat miaowing.

Olivia Pinkham (8)
St Helen's School, Northwood

Up The Stairs

Today I went up the stairs. I thought that
someone would be waiting. Then I saw a ghost. I
didn't believe it at first, but then I saw my parents.
There was blood trickling down from their heads.
This ghost, it was a murderer! Oh yes! It was
Halloween today!

Lulu Hao (9)
St Helen's School, Northwood

Monsters On Halloween

Georgia was walking home on Halloween. Suddenly, out of the corner of her eye, she saw four monsters approaching her. Georgia was frightened. Then, thankfully, three of them took off their monster masks! They were only her family! But who was the other monster? This one was holding a knife!

Jenna Karim
St Helen's School, Northwood

Scooby-Doo And The Luminous Monster!

'Now we will wait for the monster!' Fred announced, after completing his ingenious trap. From nowhere the luminous monsters rose from behind the crate.

'Now!' Daphne screamed and lowered the net, but Scooby yelped and the monster chased him! Miraculously it slipped and Shaggy crept out. Velma uncovered the monster's mask …

Aparna Arya (11)
St Helen's School, Northwood

Sophie's Travels

Sophie was flying home from Canada, when
British Airways went on strike. Her family
slept on their bags overnight. The rest of the
passengers went home. The next morning the
plane was running and ready to go. They almost
missed it, finally they jumped on. Sophie was
home again.

Amelia Murphy (11)
St Helen's School, Northwood

The Approacher

Emma was walking home from her piano lesson
late at night. She saw a car parked outside her
house but her parents were out all weekend. A
man's head popped out of the window and in
his hand was a knife, he crept out of the car and
approached Emma …

Susanna O'Connor (10)
St Helen's School, Northwood

149

The Lost Island

'Ahoy me hearties, shiver me timbers,' Violet said.
'You cold?' Klaus asked.
'No it doesn't matter, look there's a long-lost
island,' Violet exclaimed.
'Wow!' Sunny said.
'Look, Sunny just said her first words,' Violet told
Klaus.
'No one cares. We're going to be rich and
famous!' Klaus answered back.

Madeline Dipple (11)
St Helen's School, Northwood

Hawaii Evacuation

When I went to Hawaii for a three week holiday,
our villa we were staying in, was built on a
dormant volcano. One day, we saw the volcano
exploding, it was erupting! We warned the closest
news centre so everyone could evacuate. Nancy
Drew saved the day!

Sophie Little (10)
St Helen's School, Northwood

The Monster Within

Darkness swept over the house. Moonlight flowed through the window, brightening up my pale, blue face. My heart pounded vigorously as I made my way up into the manor. A dark figure shuffled through the darkness. Cautiously, I followed him into the room. I saw fangs. It was all over.

Gayatree Amalananda (10)
St Helen's School, Northwood

The Two Little Ghosts And A Pig

He went to the door on his little trotters and
opened it ever so slowly, to find that there was
only a ghostly outline of his brothers there. *'Argh!'*
he screamed as he shut the door behind him.
He opened the door again, and a voice shrieked,
'Boo!'

Sofiya Anwar (10)
St Helen's School, Northwood

Invasion!

Last night the world was quiet. Suddenly, *'Crash!'*
I walked outside to see a giant, silver spaceship.
Inside sat a green, shiny creature with big, bulging
eyes. I yelled and ran straight back into my house.
'I thought aliens didn't exist!'
I ran upstairs and saw the alien standing there …

Pooja Patel (10)
St Helen's School, Northwood

The Ride!

Katie's friends arrived for her birthday party at Alton Towers. They hopped into a bus. When they arrived, they paid for their tickets. After that, they got into a carriage for a ride in the dark. *Screech!* The carriage halted, a voice boomed from the speaker. It was Death …

Simran Dhorda (10)
St Helen's School, Northwood

The Day I Became A Millionaire

It was Easter Monday when Mother bought me the biggest horse in the world. It went in the Guinness Book of Records and I became I millionaire. Mum was over the moon and from that day on she was always there for me. My mum is the best mum ever!

Juenelle Muge (10)
St Helen's School, Northwood

The Attic

Rosie crept up to the attic, it was dark. She flicked
a switch to turn the light on, but it wouldn't.
She was sure when she came up that morning it
worked.
The light flicked on, Rosie screamed.
'It's me!' her dad said.
'Oh, I flicked on the wrong switch!'

Priya Patel (11)
St Helen's School, Northwood

157

The Disco

It was a stormy night. Kelly was ready to go to the
disco. There was a knock at the door. *It's Brad,*
Kelly thought. At the door was a man in a long,
black cloak. He grabbed Kelly and carried her
through the foggy rain. She was never seen again.

Isobel Shaw (11)
St Helen's School, Northwood

Blood

'Let's play hide-and-seek,' Katie exclaimed.
'Sure,' Poppie replied.
It was Halloween and the girls were in vampire
costumes, but people didn't know that Katie had
a secret. Katie had found Poppie, but as Poppie
stepped up a bite ran down her neck and blood
came from Katie's mouth …

Tenisha Pandya (10)
St Helen's School, Northwood

A Trip To The Woods

I walked into the woods. I was looking for my
sister. She was lost again. As I tiptoed in, a gust
of wind whipped my hair all over my face, I was
alone at last. Just as I started homewards, a girl
tapped me on the shoulder … 'Here I am!'

Olivia Braun (10)
St Helen's School, Northwood

The Pier

It was twenty years ago to this day that I did the worst thing ever.
It was a Wednesday, I was going out with Poppy. We were at the pier and I pushed her, only for a joke, she fell screaming. I had just killed my best friend ever …

Penelope Pomroy (10)
St Helen's School, Northwood

The Girl In The Garden!

It's a gloomy night, and this girl is chucking stones at my window! Who is she? What is she doing here? Oh my gosh, I do know her, she is a girl I met in the supermarket! Shall I go down or not? But what will Mum say?

Emily Bickerstaff (10)
St Helen's School, Northwood

162

Halloween

Maya stepped into the haunted house. A number of ghosts jumped out at her. Maya screamed and fell down onto a roller coaster. The roller coaster was going so fast. Things were jumping out at Maya. Finally the ride came to an end. Maya thought the ride had been great.

Maya Kateli (8)
St Helen's School, Northwood

Goldilocks On Roller Skates

One day there was a girl called Goldilocks, she
had a friend. They went for a stroll. 'But don't go
through the woods,' she said. Goldilocks went
on her roller skates. She ate some ice cream and
then she went home but she tripped on Daddy
Bear's foot. She got eaten!

Molly Thompson (9)
St Helen's School, Northwood

Tasha's Sunny Day!

Tasha crept into the big scary garden. 'Help!' she shouted as she fell down a dark, deep hole! 'Oh look fairies, pixies and elves with a bright gleam of the sun!' Suddenly there was a puff of smoke and Tasha turned into a fairy! She loved it!

Tasha Neelakandan (7)
St Helen's School, Northwood

Dreams Will Never Come True

I was in my comfy bed dreaming about breathtaking stories that I wish could happen throughout time. Suddenly I woke up from my dream, my eyes as wide open as an owl. A man came out of the wardrobe. His skull dripping blood, could that happen in real life stories?

Charlotte Messias (9)
St Helen's School, Northwood

The Creepy Trip

One day a school went to a haunted house. They stepped in and screamed like mad. Another girl went into a room with ghosts and monsters. The monsters had sharp knives and the ghosts had scary guns. With one shot she died on the floor.

Nyah Patel (8)
St Helen's School, Northwood

The Creepy House

Millie slowly crept into the living room and she couldn't find the light but suddenly the light went on. She ran upstairs and went in the bathroom to hide. 'I wish Mummy was here.'

Millie Patel (7)
St Helen's School, Northwood

168

Sleepover

Elle's friends were coming for a sleepover. But she had a secret that she was scared of the dark. When Ella's friends came to her house, they slept in a tent. When they slept in it, Ella was scared, though she had her friends and she wasn't scared anymore.

Tanvi Vaghjiani (8)
St Helen's School, Northwood

Mermaid

Once upon a time there was a mermaid called
Aquamarine. She had blue hair and bright green
eyes. She longed for true love. Every time she
wanted true love she would lose a scale. She
wanted to leave the water. One day she saw true
love, she was truly amazed.

Ope Adegbite (10)
St Helen's School, Northwood

The Creepy House

Amy walked along the street. She saw a very strange door. It was shaped as a monster. She opened the door and the house looked very strange. The house was covered in cobwebs. Suddenly, she saw a shadow, Amy got very scared, it looked like a person. 'Hello,' whispered someone.

Caitlin Smithers (8)
St Helen's School, Northwood

The Shark Of Death

Sofia slowly into the deep, dark sea. As she jumped in, suddenly a shark caught her leg! Sofia screamed and screamed! Then suddenly her mum heard, she rushed down the beach and jumped into the sea, but she did not make it on time. Sofia was dead!

Doluwa Bolaji (7)
St Helen's School, Northwood

172

Young Girl In Scary House

One day a girl called Alice was stretching out
her arms and was getting out of bed. That girl
was very pretty. Alice walked downstairs. Alice
was amazed at what she saw. She saw creepy
monsters, then her parents jumped out at her and
said, 'Trick or treat?'

Hana Lalani (8)
St Helen's School, Northwood

Grandma's Haunted House

As Olivia slowly crept into her Grandma's house, the lights flickered and in a few seconds it was pitch-black. She saw a bright light through a crack in the door, and footsteps coming from it. The door opened, it was Grandma. 'Trick or treat?' she said, laughing a lot!

Micaela Infante (9)
St Helen's School, Northwood

The Lost Cat

One day there was a cat that was weak, tired, hungry and thirsty. It was so weak it fainted. A while later a girl was passing by, she saw the cat so she took the cat home. She put the cat on a bed and looked after it.

Chor Yeen Fung
St Helen's School, Northwood

Flitz

Flitz walked slowly down the smooth, gold road of Pixwood Town. It was her glorious thirteenth birthday. She was wondering what she would get for her birthday. She was right outside her toadstool when she heard a big, enormous dash! When Flitz went inside the toadstool … 'Surprise!' screamed Flitz's friends.

Amee Shah (8)
St Helen's School, Northwood

The Tooth Fairy

One night Jessie, a young girl, had lost her tooth. She was so happy that she went to bed extra early. She put her tooth under her pillow and she waited for the tooth fairy. Then she came. When Jessie woke up she found a shiny £1. She was happy.

Clarissa Milkowski (9)
St Helen's School, Northwood

Boo!

Pix the pixie had found a secret way through the garden into the house. He sat on the table eating lettuce, when he saw a shadow on the wall. 'Monster!' he cried. He sprinted away and hid under the clock. The monster came closer and squeaked. It was a mouse!

Doyin Bolaji (9)
St Helen's School, Northwood

Help!

Amy knocked on her friend's door and it flew open. She walked into a room and found a ghost wandering around and a vampire walking up the stairs. She ran out screaming and the door slammed behind her. She was terrified and where was her friend? Wait … Oh no!

Charlotte Sawyer (9)
St Helen's School, Northwood

The Walking Sugar Lump

Once upon a time a walking sugar lump was in his room reading a book about his world, Lump World. Suddenly he leant against his wall and fell through it! He found himself in England! The sugar lump started worrying. Then suddenly he was back in Sugar Lump World, wow!

Anna Kordo (9)

St Helen's School, Northwood

The Talking Bubble Bath

One day a girl, Rachel, was called by her mother to get in the bubble bath. So Rachel slowly walked upstairs and got in. Suddenly, as she got in, she heard small voices. She looked down and there were the bubbles, talking! She woke up, it was a dream, phew.

Caitlin McDermott (9)
St Helen's School, Northwood

Cliffhanger

I decided to hang off a tall mountain. I took my
friend, he helped me to get up the mountain and
hang off. Then he said, 'Boo!' I was gone. All that
was left of me was my broken bones!

Georgia Machado (9)
St Helen's School, Northwood

182

The Magic Kingdom

On a cold, wet, damp night, a boy called Sam was walking on the road with his friend Jack. They were dripping wet from head to toe. They went home on the bus to get new clothes, suddenly they were in the Magic Kingdom!

Yasmine Shaikh (8)
St Helen's School, Northwood

The Chocolate Bar

One day a girl went to the chocolate shop with her mother in her tomato-red coloured car. When she'd bought the chocolate bar, she tore it open and bit ravenously into it. Suddenly she spat out half of the eaten chocolate and handed it back to the shopkeeper!

Alice Johnstone (10)
St Helen's School, Northwood

A Little Girl

In a small town there was a big house. In the big house there was a little girl. That girl was not like any ordinary girl, in fact she was an extraordinary girl. She was good at gym, singing, playing instruments, dancing, maths, English, science, art and games!

Lauren Morton (7)
St Helen's School, Northwood

Night Before Christmas

It was the night before Christmas, Kate was
about to fall asleep, if it weren't for those echoing
footsteps walking down the narrow hallway. She
got up, dazed and disorientated. However Kate
did hear the heavy *thud* downstairs near the
Christmas tree. She went downstairs, seeing a
Christmas present thief!

Olivia Paes (9)
St Helen's School, Northwood

186

The Birthday Surprise

A little boy, Karim, didn't know we were going to throw a birthday surprise. We got a big chocolate cake and lots of presents. When he came downstairs we all shouted, 'Surprise!' He was so happy he blew out the candles and ripped open the biggest present first!

Alisha Janmohamed (8)
St Helen's School, Northwood

Old Grandma Muffet

Old Grandma Muffet stood on her tuffet on
a sparkly, starry night. Suddenly fire appeared
with a fright, that's when she feared to act like a
knight. So there she was, marching down the hill
with her saucepan and spoon, saying filled with
pride, 'How brave am I this afternoon!'

Tabitha Shannon (9)
St Helen's School, Northwood

188

My Little Brother And The Curse Of The Easter Egg

I stepped into the kitchen, to find my brother
stuffing himself with eggs. *What a pig!* I thought.
One day he will turn into an egg! I moved away
from my thoughts to an amazing sight. Too late!
He's gone. Well, I'm looking forward to that big
egg! My brother!

Lilian Cottrell (10)

St Helen's School, Northwood

Happy Birthday Tooth Fairy

Once upon a time there lived a tooth fairy who
was going to a very creepy house, to drop off the
one pound and pick up a tooth.
When she arrived at the house she was very
scared because the house was dark. When she
opened the door - 'Happy birthday!'

Eleanor Burling (9)
St Helen's School, Northwood

190

Untitled

This blood-eating vampire lived with Sweeny Todd the barber. Nobody ever wanted to go into the cave where they lurked around. At Halloween people dared each other to go in the cave and so Molly and David crept in. They discovered the two children and ... suddenly they were dead!

Arrianne Whittick (9)
St Helen's School, Northwood

You've Been April Fooled

It's April Fool's Day and fairy Kirsty and fairy
Rachel are going to the fairy café to get away
from the goblins that don't leave the fairies alone.
Rachel fairy gets in a goblin costume secretly and
jumps out, shocking fairy Kirsty. 'You've been
April fooled!'

Tazmin Racke (8)
St Helen's School, Northwood

Flutterfairy's Friends

One night, Flutterfairy was busy making dresses
for the wonder ball and just couldn't stay awake.
Flutterfairy had been sewing little trinkets and
beads onto beautiful dresses. Then Flutterfairy
decided she had to have just a wink of sleep.
After an hour her friends came and finished them
off beautifully!

Simran Lakha (9)
St Helen's School, Northwood

Wonder Hole

Alfie went into the living room. Alfie went to a door, he opened it. Inside was the Arctic. He found a polar bear. At first the polar bear bit him, then they became friends and the polar bear gave him a lift home and Alfie agreed to come again very soon.

Ishani Patwal (7)
St Helen's School, Northwood

194

Herbie And Violet Veronica

Once upon a time, on the Isle of Sweets, Herbie the chocolate bar was taking a stroll, when he heard Violet Veronica scream!
'Argh!' Violet Veronica shouted. 'Herbie, help!' she shouted again. Violet Veronica was shouting because Elf had given her a terrible fright. Elf had turned into a tarantula!

Natalia Ghandi Burnett (9)
St Helen's School, Northwood

The Voice

I search for Jack. My family predicts he is dead but I don't believe them as I hear his voice every now and then. I need to find him, I can't live without him. It is like his voice is getting closer … I hear a voice lurking underground …

Reeya Shah (11)
St Helen's School, Northwood

196

A New Light

Boom! More bombs from above explode.
Everyone scrambles into Mrs Lee's preserved
WWII shelter. 'What'll happen if WWIII breaks
out?' Karren whispered, but there was no answer.
As she clambered into the shelter Karren saw
a shimmering light, the light's colour was a
wonderful sight like a clear, blue sky.

Shreya Patel (11)
St Helen's School, Northwood

Untitled

One stormy night, the windows shattered, the floor was creaky and there was a horrible cackle. Suddenly, the door opened, a skeleton crept in. The skeleton walked through the door into the kitchen, up the stairs and into the bedroom and it was coming up to me …
'Argh!' I screamed.

Tara Das (8)
St Helen's School, Northwood

The Adventure

I went down the stairs and out the door. I said, 'Bye, Mum,' and I hugged her. I was on an adventure to see if I could find the flower that everyone has tried to find, including my next-door neighbour, James Patterson.

Hannah Bayes (9)
St Helen's School, Northwood

Untitled

I went upstairs, then downstairs, where was my mum? Where was Dad? Then I opened the door and I saw blood! Lying there were my mum and dad. 'Mum!' I screamed. 'Dad!' There was no answer. All I heard was the wind. I rushed downstairs. I rang 911. *Bang* ...

Anya Patel (8)
St Helen's School, Northwood

The Ghost House

The house was pitch-black and the door creaked.
'Hello?' whispered Molly looking at the door
nervously. There was no answer. Molly went back
to watching TV. The creak came again. Molly sat
straight up. 'Who's there?' she asked. 'I said who's
there?' Nobody answered. 'Mum are you back?'

Maya Das (10)
St Helen's School, Northwood

Cuddles, The Little Bear

It was a sunny day and Cuddles the bear was out in his garden collecting honey from a beehive. It started to rain so Cuddles went inside and ate his honey with a big plate of cookies. Cuddles was full and tired so he went to sleep very peacefully.

Catherine Tadena (10)
St Helen's School, Northwood

202

The Worst Ever Parents' Evening

'Tom's a ghastly boy,' said Mrs Jones.
'Don't be mean,' his dad said.
'He bullies kids!' she argued back.
Tom's dad punched her.
'Security!' cried Mrs Jones frantically. 'Call the police!' She dialled 999.
'He's supposed to be in jail,' said the policeman.
'We'll never know how he cleverly escaped.'

Lucy Evans (10)
St Helen's School, Northwood

Jungle Nightmare

Rose stepped into the luscious jungle. She hopped over all the leaves and sticks. 'Rose, Rose, where are you?' came a voice from the distance. Rose hadn't heard the voice, she was stunned as the white lion approached her, but lightning struck Rose and she dropped down dead.

Sophie Fung (10)
St Helen's School, Northwood

Untitled

One day there lived a girl called Emma. She lived in an orphanage. Her dream was to get adopted by a family. That night she dreamed that the next morning her mum would come. The next morning there was a knock at the door, standing there was her mum.

Natasha Robin (10)
St Helen's School, Northwood

The Painting That Came Alive

'At last I have finished my painting,' said Sophie.
Suddenly the picture got out of the canvas. The
picture started to itch its leg.
'Why are you itching yourself? It looks weird,' said
Sophie.
He took a knife and slowly plunged it into her
kind, loving, thoughtful heart.

Sara Goldstein (9)
St Helen's School, Northwood

Holly's Birthday

It was Holly's birthday and her mum and dad were not there. She heard a bird singing like Dad and another singing like Mum. They went inside. Holly ran upstairs, she got her box and asked, 'Can I have my mum and dad back?' They came back in a whoosh.

Charlotte Robin (7)
St Helen's School, Northwood

The Adventure He Never Forgot

The cold winter breeze stung William's cheek. His teeth chattered as he stumbled on. He soon came across a dark cave and he lay down to rest. Suddenly he heard the sound of something panting. Looking outside he saw a pack of fearsome-looking dogs. 'Great,' he muttered angrily. 'Wolves.'

Charis Umerah (8)
St Helen's School, Northwood

The Lone Dog

It's always a dark mysterious night when the lone dog is out. He howls at the moon at the wettest times. He sometimes goes up to owners but they kick him out. So now he lives in the dump, praying to have someone who loves him with all their heart.

Tilly Hedges (8)
St Helen's School, Northwood

Easter Egg Or Crunchy Carrot?

Hop, hop went Rabbit as she nibbled on the
crunchy carrot. She heard children laughing.
She looked up. They gave her an Easter egg.
She glanced at her carrot. It was not there! She
nibbled the chocolate egg. It tasted better than
carrots! 'I'll be the Easter bunny!' she exclaimed.

Rachel Gardner (8)
St Helen's School, Northwood

The Easter Bunny Is Found

It was night-time when the Easter bunny was found. A girl awoke to a loud bang. Eggs were cascading out of a bag. When at last it stopped, underneath the eggs lay the Easter bunny. 'No! You found me. Don't tell anybody.'
'I won't,' whispered the girl.

Victoria Catherall (10)
St Helen's School, Northwood

Last Catch

It was a stormy night, he was walking around the block, identity unknown, with a dagger behind his back and sweets in his hand. That was the last catch, a small, little girl. There she was, strolling across the road, by herself, in the dark, stormy night. His last chance.

Sasha Meghani (10)
St Helen's School, Northwood

Easter Bunny

It was Saturday at last, what all the kids had been waiting for for ages. Some children were meeting up to have an Easter egg hunt. Finally they were ready to start the Easter egg hunt. When the children were doing the hunt, a strange voice started to chase them!

Francesca Wall (9)
St Helen's School, Northwood

My Angel, Angelica

Angelica was my best friend. I was used to
agreeing with her until that fateful day when
she was in the road, and then a car. A squeal of
brakes. A scream. Silence. She was a perfect
friend to me and remains in my heart, but she's
an angel now.

Precious Kufeji (11)
St John Fisher Primary School, Perivale

214

Finding Her

I hated having my birthdays at the home. I didn't mind being an orphan, I just loathed the birthdays. I took a deep breath as I opened the door. Everyone started singing 'Happy birthday'. However, a woman had caught my eye. She looked familiar. Maybe she was … surely not? Mum?

Patrycja Piotrowska (11)
St John Fisher Primary School, Perivale

Being Followed

I kept running. I didn't know if he was still behind me. I knew by now I'd lost him. I ran home. The house was dark. Not a thing moved. I was worried. I slowly crept in. The door creaked. I went in … I fainted, seeing my stalker. *Run!*

Victoria Chmielewski (10)
St John Fisher Primary School, Perivale

Loud To Quiet

Mia was a loud girl. She would never stop
shouting. Then one day, her mum and dad left her
at home.
That night she watched horror movies. Then she
heard a voice: 'Mia, you have to be quiet 'cause
your mum is pregnant.' She nearly never shouted
again!

Gemma Murray (10)
St John Fisher Primary School, Perivale

The Knock

Kelly was watching TV in the living room when she suddenly heard a knock on the door. Who could it be? *Knock, knock, knock*, again, but everyone was out. Slowly, she crept across the room, looked out of the window and laughed with relief. Ben had forgotten his keys!

Niamh Meehan (11)
St John Fisher Primary School, Perivale

Knock, Knock

Knock, knock. Emily's friends arrived for her sleepover - Lucy and Sarah, her best friends. Unfortunately, there was a disaster, she had burnt the food. Luckily, her mum popped round unexpectedly. What a relief. Emily's mum went and bought them a pizza. Emily and her friends had the best sleepover ever.

Louise Botti (11)
St John Fisher Primary School, Perivale

It Won't Be Fine!

I walk through the cold, dreary city, wishing
everything will be alright. But it won't. Never.
It will all end soon. I will get the operation and
everything will be fine, I hope.
'You will be fine! Listen to me!' shouts Evelin.
But I don't think I will …

Stephanie Tubbritt (10)
St John Fisher Primary School, Perivale

220

My Brother Is A Demon

Ding-dong! There was nobody there. I closed the door. There it was, the demon! 'Leave!' I told him. He wouldn't. I screamed for Mum. She said it was nothing and I should calm down. Turned out my brother that died was the demon. He's been tracking me down since.

Stephanie Mansour (11)
St John Fisher Primary School, Perivale

Seconds To React

We took off from London to LA. A little boy
looked under his seat. 'It's a bomb!'
The first class in the plane was evacuated to
economy. Another kid came back to fiddle with
the bomb in the box. 'I wonder what's in it?' He
pressed the 'eject' button …
'Peek-a-boo!'

Joshua Bimpong (11)
St John Fisher Primary School, Perivale

222

Witch

On a cold, rainy day, three children wanted to go outside. Their parents said no. They pleaded so the parents said, 'Yes, but beware of the witch.' The children were playing outside having fun until they heard a scary laugh. It was the witch, who kidnapped them. The end?

Sasan Ghareman-Nejad
St John Fisher Primary School, Perivale

The Loud Noise

Grace was on her way home when she heard
a noise. She got scared. She didn't know what
to do, so she knocked on the door. A woman
answered. Grace asked, 'Who are you?'
The woman replied, 'Your soul.'
She said, 'But I'm not dead.'
She replied, 'You are now.'

Sophie Goddard (11)
St John Fisher Primary School, Perivale

Night Fright

The banging on Jenny's roof woke her up. She was petrified and quickly pulled the covers over her head. Was a burglar trying to break in through the attic? Somehow she found the courage to look out her bedroom window.

'Ho, ho, ho!' shouted Santa. 'Hope you enjoy your presents!'

Ciara Gibbs (10)
St John Fisher Primary School, Perivale

The Day My Cat Went To School

I was at school. I was in the middle of the registration when I heard something in my bag. *Miaow, miaow!* I opened it and it was a cat! On his collar it said, 'I'm Alfie, a late Christmas present'. I quickly texted my parents, 'Thank you so, so much'.

Emily O'Shea (9)
St John Fisher Primary School, Perivale

226

Er, I Dunno!

One day Burt was going to school. When he got
there he took out his pencil case and sat down.
The teacher asked him, 'What is two times two?'
Burt answered, 'Er, I dunno.'
'Gosh, learn your tables!'
On the way home some children asked him,
'What is your name …!'

Levon-Aren Minasian (10)
St John Fisher Primary School, Perivale

227

Thunder!

The wind whistled as it soared past the clouds.
Lightning stung as it flooded the skies. The storm
had begun and the demon was coming. All went
silent, tense, waiting for the scream. The pests
hid and the flowers buried their heads, afraid of
the evil that was here. Thunder!

Mairead McGovern (9)
St John Fisher Primary School, Perivale

The Knock

The house was empty. Where were my parents?
Suddenly, I heard a knock on the door. I saw
a shadow of somebody with spiky hair. I was
extremely frightened. I crept to the door and
opened it ...
'Do you like the wig for your dress-up day?' Mum
shouted loudly.

Una Alberti (10)
St John Fisher Primary School, Perivale

Mystery Man

The house looked creepy and dark. Jakub
knocked on the door. It creaked and opened.
There was nobody in. Jakub was creeped out.
Then a man came out, he was very old. The old
man asked Jakub what his name was.
He replied, 'Jakub.'
Jakub had found his grandpa.

Owen Silvester (9)
St John Fisher Primary School, Perivale

The Real Bunny

It was Easter Sunday. Molly always had an Easter
egg hunt. She raced downstairs in excitement.
Her parents left the puzzle notes for solving.
She followed the clues into the garden. At last,
spotting a small box, Molly peered inside. There
stood a real, fluffy Easter bunny!

Megan Nee (9)
St John Fisher Primary School, Perivale

Medusa

Long ago, after the Trojan war, there lived the
Gorgon. She killed people with her eyes.
One day Perseus wanted to fight her. He saw
some women on the way, so he asked them for
some advice. He went to Medusa, chopped her
head off and was known as king.

Nicole Frankiewicz (9)
St John Fisher Primary School, Perivale

Where's My Cat?

When me and my mum came home, we went
to see my cat. He was usually on my bed or in
the shed, so we went to look in those places. He
wasn't there so we were worried. We walked
into the kitchen and found him in the cupboard!

Rebecca McLoughlin (9)
St John Fisher Primary School, Perivale

Christmas Night

It was Christmas Eve. A noise suddenly woke
me. I went downstairs. I turned on the lights and
looked out the window, where I saw Santa riding
away shouting, 'Ho, ho, ho!' I went back to sleep.
In the morning my parents were billionaires,
thanks for Santa's fake money!

Kieran Rice (10)
St John Fisher Primary School, Perivale

234

Spring

There were two bunches of daffodils on the table waiting for a vase. I thought I would help my mum by putting the daffodils in a vase so they could grow. An hour later, flowers opened, but only one bunch of flowers opened. I thought, *it had no water!*

Uden Henry (10)
St John Fisher Primary School, Perivale

Mum's Hot Sauce

I came into the house and saw piles of red on the
floor. It could only mean one terrible thing - the
worst day of the week, Mum was cooking! Trust
me, every time Mum cooks red-hot salsa sauce. I
sniffed - *argh!* Mum had put extra spices in!

Sorcha Walsh (10)
St John Fisher Primary School, Perivale

The Birthday Surprise

One night James walked into a room. It was dull and dark. When he turned around he saw a man had jumped over the fence. James went outside and the man was his dad. They went inside and his mum jumped out with a cake. This was the best surprise!

James Botti (9)
St John Fisher Primary School, Perivale

The Ocean

It was the first day of the summer holidays and I was swimming in the ocean with my friend, Abby. I was looking at the beautiful coral reef when I saw a shark swimming towards me. I wanted to swim away, but I heard Abby's voice, 'Like my scary costume?'

Magda Zalewa (10)
St John Fisher Primary School, Perivale

Runaway

I listened carefully to my parents. I could hear
screaming and shouting from upstairs. I couldn't
take it anymore, this happened too many times.
As I packed my bag with food and clothes, I was
ready for my getaway. As I was walking, I felt
frightened …

Gabriella Atlabachew (11)
St John Fisher Primary School, Perivale

A Nightmare To Remember

My mother sings a lullaby. I kiss goodbye, my breathing heavy as I go into a deep sleep. I hear the sound of screaming and shouting, a blurred picture in my head. I drown with my hands against my heart.
I wake suddenly! That was a nightmare to remember!

Dhara Fernando (11)
St John Fisher Primary School, Perivale

Bad Hermon

Once there was a boy called Hermon who didn't like work. At school, two boys called Dom and Dan told the teacher of him.
On Monday she called him in and told him that he was in Friday club. Then he went and got in trouble, then went home.

Hermon Elias (10)
St John Fisher Primary School, Perivale

My Friend, Biscuit

I once had a friend, he was a biscuit. We always
played with each other day and night, until one
terrible thing happened. Someone flushed it down
the toilet. I was sad day and night, with no one to
play with when out of the toilet came my friend,
Biscuit.

Dominic Starzynski (10)
St John Fisher Primary School, Perivale

242

Oh, The Weather

Sunshine, glorious sunshine, that's the weather
today. I have heard the forecast - a hot 20°C.
Sunbathing on the beach, licking vanilla ice
cream drizzled with strawberry sauce, drinking
refreshing, tangy lemonade and just relaxing. I
can't wait.
I jump out of bed, draw the curtains - it's raining!

Michaela Tranfield (10)
St John Fisher Primary School, Perivale

Forget, Lose, Whatever!

Ping! A pen appeared in front of Alex. He picked it up and started to write. *Ping!* Incredibly, he went forward in time. He was now at school and hadn't done his homework. His teacher asked the class for homework. 'Alex?'
'I forgot it, I lost it, whatever!'
'Detention!'

Ben Chesters (11)
St John Fisher Primary School, Perivale

244

The Killer!

Julia lived with her grandmother in a castle. Two
weeks later her grandmother died.
On Sunday, Julia was walking around the castle.
Her feet crept on the floorboards. Suddenly a
rush of wind tackled her neck. She saw it! She
saw it! *The killer!* Julia died two weeks later.

Jessica Krafczyk (11)
St John Fisher Primary School, Perivale

245

I Forget!

I woke up at seven, had a shower at half-past,
changed at fifteen to, waited for something. I was
sitting down waiting. My mum came in, tired and
went to bed. She woke up. 'Kevin, what are you
doing?'
Then I said, 'Er, don't know Mum, I forget!'

Femi Roche (11)
St John Fisher Primary School, Perivale

Birthday Fright

The window's closed, even though the wind's coming through, knocking under the dark bed. I can hear footsteps coming upstairs. What can I do? I'm scared stiff. I can't put my head under the covers. I see a small light …
'Boo!' It's only Dad wishing me a happy birthday.

Vanja Simonovic (11)
St John Fisher Primary School, Perivale

The Happy Fly

The mosquito buzzed brightly through the air, diving and enjoying its freedom, happily zipping around, seeing a delicious lizard full of blood. It sets its tail and wings and dive-bombs it. *Snap!* Its flight has come to a sticky end thanks to the frog's tongue. 'Nice to eat you!'

Elena Joseph (11)
St John Fisher Primary School, Perivale

Football Crazy

Kevin was in the football team and everyone was teasing him because he wasn't scoring goals. He tried and tried. Today, he tried and tried so hard, he scored eleven goals! Everyone was so happy. Everyone congratulated him for hours upon hours. Everyone said sorry to Kevin and celebrated victory.

Kevin Boje (10)
St John Fisher Primary School, Perivale

249

No Electricity For The Night

As we entered the house, Mum turned on the light, but it didn't work. But it wasn't only us, it was the neighbours as well. So we gave them candles and we lit one for ourselves. We didn't have electricity until the next evening. No electricity for the whole night!

Trinity Lam (9)
St John Fisher Primary School, Perivale

250

The Terrifying Creeps

In a house where it was all dark, there was always a sudden creep.
When a girl came home she heard a sudden creep. She was petrified, she didn't know what to do. She heard another creep. It was louder and louder and then … stopped!

Talitha Ferdinand (9)
St John Fisher Primary School, Perivale

Afraid

Bethany, Sarah and Anexy were walking down the road. The bushes started shaking and they were scared. They huddled together in a ball.
'Boo!' Out jumped Michael who had scared them all along!

Jassica Kaniude (10)
St John Fisher Primary School, Perivale

Everyone Is Asleep

As Millie went up the stairs, she heard a scary
sound. Then she fell and there was a big bang.
Millie didn't make it though. She carried on going
up the stairs. When she reached the top, she
stumbled into a room. She screamed very loudly.
Everyone was awake now!

Lauren McNevin (9)
St John Fisher Primary School, Perivale

The Haunted House

As Kate went in the haunted house there was a white shroud around it. She entered and walked to an unusual, dusty old brown door. She opened it and it creaked loudly. Kate saw a horrific sight in the dark room. It was a monster ...
It was all a dream!

Deepa Kumaran (10)
St John Fisher Primary School, Perivale

The Mouse

As morning came, a mouse approached. As usual
she went up the wall. Suddenly she heard a crack.
She turned around and saw a hole. She went into
it and looked around.
The next day she got all her things and made her
home there.

Weronika Baranowska (10)
St John Fisher Primary School, Perivale

Stealing Is Bad

I go into the cloakroom and I see my friend
stealing money out of children's pockets. I don't
know what to do. I go to him but then I stop and
know what to do. I get home, take my bag off and
pray for my friend to stop.

Karol Fryzlewicz (10)
St John Fisher Primary School, Perivale

The Big Surprise

When Mr Crossland opened the door, the most
disgusting sight greeted him - monsters with
warts, vampires with fangs, hellhounds with big,
old, greasy horns.
'Ukk!' said Mr Crossland in a whisper.
'Happy Halloween.'
What a surprise it was. Then Mr Crossland gave
the monsters lots of juicy fruit - yuck!

Jordan Victor (9)
St John Fisher Primary School, Perivale

Exam Trouble

Angelica was a pretty, clever, sweet girl who loved nature. Her best friend, Kate, was the exact opposite. There were exams and Kate needed to study, so Angelica offered to help. They went to the library every day. The exams came and went. Kate got an A, Angelica a D!

Isobel Grundy (10)
St John Fisher Primary School, Perivale

No Fish

There was once a man who went fishing every
day so his family could eat.
One day his net caught nothing. He didn't get any
fish, so he decided to put on diving clothes and
see what the problem was. But the fish were just
scared of his boat!

Rannan Cunningham (9)
St John Fisher Primary School, Perivale

Maria's Brother

It was a bright day and Maria was in her garden. There, in a corner, was a dinosaur. Maria ran! Maria then recognised the voice. It was in fact her brother all dressed up ready for school because it was dressing-up day. Maria and her brother could not stop laughing.

Anexy Antonykumar (9)
St John Fisher Primary School, Perivale

Ashamed

Sam was walking in the park when he saw a man with bloody teeth walking up to him. Sam closed his eyes, then opened his eyes. He was right in front of him. He said, 'Is there any money for the poor?'
Sam felt so ashamed. He walked away.

Andre Lopes (10)
St John Fisher Primary School, Perivale

My Surprise Birthday

It was my birthday. I went to school, but no one said happy birthday. I had told them when my birthday was. If they didn't say happy birthday, I didn't want to be friends. Suddenly there was an assembly. When I went to assembly, they all shouted, 'Happy birthday!'

Dilmith Weerasinghe (9)
St John Fisher Primary School, Perivale

The Mystery

I was at the shops. My mum told me she would meet me at the uninteresting clothing row. I went there but I couldn't see her. I checked everywhere. Everybody was looking at me. I went to the cashier and …
'My favourite video game. Thanks Mum!' I was extremely joyful!

Marcel Hadad (9)
St John Fisher Primary School, Perivale

Mandy In The Olympics

There was a girl called Mandy, she liked running.
She begged her mum to go to the Olympics. She
said yes.
When it was the race, she lost. A girl called Chloe
won. Then she said, 'Well done. You tried your
best. At least you are second.'

Mandy Vangu (9)
St John Fisher Primary School, Perivale

Rhianna's Halloween

Rhianna opened her eyes. It was dark. She heard
a creak. Something moved in the corridor. She
tried to put the light on, it didn't work! Suddenly,
the doors opened, the light switched on ...
'Happy Halloween!'
What a surprise party! thought Rhianna.

Dorota Dziki (10)
St John Fisher Primary School, Perivale

Untitled

It was dark, the stars glittered like diamonds in the calm night. Everyone in our house was asleep, except for the crying of our family cat. She wouldn't settle, something was not right. I came down the stairs. I slowly went into the kitchen … There lay four kittens, sleeping peacefully!

Marcus Browne (10)

St John Fisher Primary School, Perivale

A Strange Sea Atmosphere

My goggles fitted my eyes perfectly as I dived into
the depths of the warm, clear water. Splashing
about amongst the brightly coloured tropical fish,
I narrowly missed a bull shark! Suddenly, I felt
myself being yanked towards a whirring
whirlpool …
Shame! My dad had pulled the bath plug out!

Benjamin Shipman (10)
St John Fisher Primary School, Perivale

Knock, Knock

Knock, knock! Someone was at the broken door.
Eleana opened the door. She was greeted by a fat
boy. There was blood dripping all over his green
teeth and hairy body. Eleana screamed, 'Oh my
days! You look terrible!'

'I know. It's Halloween. Trick or treat?' John (her
brother) replied.

Georgia Whaley (11)
St John Fisher Primary School, Perivale

The Wolf In The Forest

Once there was a little girl going through the forest in the middle of the night. In a matter of seconds, a wolf attacked her, then she started to cry. She slipped her hand on the wolf's head and took the mask off. It was her brother!

David Olenski (10)
St John Fisher Primary School, Perivale

I Like It!

Robert got to the hairdresser's. At first he gave
Robert spikes, but he didn't like it, so he made
his hair very short, but Robert still didn't like it.
So the hairdresser tried 50 more cuts and then
Robert didn't have any hair left!
'I like it!' he said.

Ania Dziki (10)
St John Fisher Primary School, Perivale

Holidays

Once upon a time there lived a child called Alex.
His two sisters were going to a camp for the
holidays. Alex went to his friend and asked him if
he could sleep over at his house.
After the holidays, the sisters came back. Alex
said, 'Great to see you!'

Karol Sobkowicz (10)
St John Fisher Primary School, Perivale

Snow White

There was a girl called Snow White. Her terrible stepmum wanted to get rid of her. She called a man to kill her, but she killed him and was rescued. The prince never found his princess, so he died all alone and never found anyone.

Sarah Goncalves (9)

St John Fisher Primary School, Perivale

272

Schooldays

First of all I would just like to say that schooldays
make me want to throw up! They are really, really
boring. I wish that there were more, and longer,
playtimes. Some lessons are boring, but some are
fun.

David Rocha (10)
St John Fisher Primary School, Perivale

Untitled

Once upon a time there was a boy called
Michael and he had two sisters called Clara and
Evangelina. They lived in a town called Alperton.
They were as poor as poor can be. They still
went to school.
Michael heard something in the cloakroom.
Robert was stealing …

Michael Yanni (10)
St John Fisher Primary School, Perivale

My Football Match

I got to my home pitch. Our manager, Bob, said if
we won, we had a chance of going up to a better
league. My dad was the ref.
Bang! The match started. We got a foul. Steven
took it. Yes! We scored! Second half, I scored.
Yes, we won!

Jake Baldry (10)
St John Fisher Primary School, Perivale

The School Of The Dead

As Molly walked into the toilets, she heard
the lightest breath of wind and the cry of an
apparition. Immediately, she turned around and
saw a white, freckled face with eyeballs rolled
backwards! Suddenly, it moved. Molly rubbed
her eyes in disbelief and saw the head teacher
chuckling deeply!

Michael Owens (8)
St Mary's Catholic Primary School, Uxbridge

A Sinking Feeling

Recently, I went to the swimming pool. I was
about to get into the water when I heard a loud
splash. I looked over and saw a body sinking to
the bottom! I ran to the side and without thinking,
I dived in. I quickly realised it was a dummy!

Erin Foley (7)
St Mary's Catholic Primary School, Uxbridge

277

The Sphinx Of Egypt

Once there was a monster called the sphinx. It had a lion's body and a woman's head. The sphinx had a riddle: it walks on 4 legs, 2, then 3. A man guessed the riddle: a man. It crawls on 4 legs, walks on 2 and uses a walking stick!

Abigail Cronin (11)
St Mary's Catholic Primary School, Uxbridge

A Shocking Tale!

It was a cold and stormy night. Jodie was walking down the dark alley leading to her house. A sudden flash of lightning made her jump. She thought she'd been struck by lightning. Then she remembered, 'Yes! My shocking tricks have arrived.'

It was her brother. *That's it!* Jodie thought.

Emma Dahl (10)
St Mary's Catholic Primary School, Uxbridge

Snow Surprise!

Zoey woke up. She felt extremely cold and started shivering. Zoey got into her school uniform and went downstairs for breakfast. Her parents were smiling at her. She wondered why. Zoey said bye to her parents and went outside. She saw a white blanket covering the ground. It was snowing!

Bethania Berhane (11)
St Mary's Catholic Primary School, Uxbridge

Soft Sand, Golden Sand

The sun shone gloriously across the golden sand,
the white-crested waves crashed onto the beach.
A solitary figure could be seen beneath the palm
trees. He appeared to be staring out to sea at the
fisherman in his boat.

Hannah sighed with contentment, the jigsaw
puzzle was finally complete.

Hannah Bohan (8)
St Mary's Catholic Primary School, Uxbridge

281

The Day I Stepped On A Leprechaun

One Saturday morning, my toast burnt in the toaster and I dropped the butter which made a dreadful mess on the kitchen floor. I poured milk into my cereal and it was sour. *Urgh!* I knew then I must have stepped on a leprechaun when I got out of bed!

Sarah Nevin
St Mary's RC Primary School, Isleworth

The Day I Nearly Fainted

On my birthday I wanted to go to the theme park. I decided to go on the biggest ride called Megamania. After I got on, I closed my eyes and was shaking so much, I thought I was going to pass out. I was so grateful when it had finished.

Katrina Nevin
St Mary's RC Primary School, Isleworth

283

Kidnapped

Hannah and her family went on holiday to Spain
where it was nice and hot. They were staying in a
hotel.
On the night they arrived, they left the door open
by accident. After the family had gone to sleep,
someone came in and kidnapped Hannah. She
was gone forever ...

Hannah Wright (11)
St Mary's RC Primary School, Isleworth

Chuckey

Chuckey went for a walk. Cars rushed beside him like they were in a hurry to get somewhere. He kept walking. He came to the crossing. Chuckey had a strange feeling something bad was going to happen …
It did. He got run over! With his last breath he whispered, 'Help!'

Imogen Wilby (11)
St Mary's RC Primary School, Isleworth

The Runaway

'Quick, the monster's coming!' James and Sean ran as fast as they could. They didn't know what to do.
'Let's go here.'
They opened a huge door. They rushed inside, locked it and stayed in there. It was pitch-black. They were cold. 'I want to go home,' Sean said …

Shechem Tesfaye
St Mary's RC Primary School, Isleworth

Facing Your Death

One night, whilst walking down an alleyway, I
heard footsteps behind me. I looked round. All I
saw was a shadow. Apprehensively, I carried on.
About five minutes later I turned again. 'Argh!
Help!' Screaming as loudly as I could, I fought the
stranger who choked me to death ...

Jennifer Samia (11)
St Mary's RC Primary School, Isleworth

Fire?

I sit bolt upright in bed, shaking and sweating
all over, after a horrible nightmare. Can I smell
smoke? *'Argh! Fire!'* It is coming from downstairs. I
run down the stairs, holding my breath. Terrified,
I look around for the fire …
Oh, there's no fire, just next-door's barbecue.
Phew!

Charlotte Doyle (10)
St Mary's RC Primary School, Isleworth

Holiday Disaster

'There's our caravan,' said Molly as Mum and Dad carried their suitcases in. Everyone stood open-mouthed. Their caravan was a mess - leaking roof and dirt and rubbish everywhere.

'We'd better clear all this up,' said Mum, looking around.

After a sleepless night, they gave up and went back home.

Ciara Foord (10)
St Mary's RC Primary School, Isleworth

The Magical Ride

Three friends went on a roundabout and jumped onto their favourite horses. Suddenly, one of these horses started making real sounds, came to life and galloped faster and faster until the roundabout stopped. When they got off, they felt quite dizzy, but happy at the same time! What a ride!

Athena Elia

St Mary's RC Primary School, Isleworth

Revenge

3C had kidnapped 3B's hamster. After finding
the ransom note, 3B sat scowling at the note
wondering what to do. After two minutes,
they decided to take revenge. They ran to the
art cupboard and took the paint. They quickly
emptied the paint into 3C's trays without any
worries!

Callum Ferguson (11)
St Mary's RC Primary School, Isleworth

Willy Wonka's Chocolate

It's 7.30am and Emma arrives at the BBC News Centre. At break time, she walks to her favourite sweet shop and buys a chocolate bar, then returns to the BBC. The boss tells her to report on Willy Wonka's poisoned chocolate. Suddenly feeling dizzy and sick, she drops down dead!

Maria Gabriel (11)
St Mary's RC Primary School, Isleworth

292

Virus

'Mum, the computer's not working,' groaned
Fred whilst hitting it. Suddenly, it whirred into life.
Then a face appeared on the screen. It started
counting backwards from fifty. When it reached
zero, it stopped. Then, *bang!*
Now that room is painted red, with blood, and
they need another family computer.

Tom O'Halloran (11)
St Mary's RC Primary School, Isleworth

293

Doomsday

As the clock struck 12 on New Year's Eve, there were celebrations going on worldwide. The fireworks began, but then they all shot into the crowd. All over the world there were things going tragically wrong. Suddenly, the whole world split in two, killing everyone!
2012 really is doomsday!

Amy Blewitt (10)
St Mary's RC Primary School, Isleworth

The Snake

It was April when things went bad. I was in a café when a python slithered out of nowhere and chased me! I screamed for help but everyone had run out. I suddenly felt a bite on my left arm and fainted, to find myself in hospital the next day.

Malika Chohan (10)
St Mary's RC Primary School, Isleworth

Jodie's Party

'Hi, come in and help yourself to food,' said Jodie.
'Here's your present,' said Sophie.
'Thanks a lot, Sophie,' Jodie replied.
Many people joined Sophie and Jodie, playing lots
of party games and eating lots of food.
'Thanks everyone for a lovely party,' said Jodie as
everyone left her house.

Jodie Geere (10)
St Mary's RC Primary School, Isleworth

Who's There?

It was a late Friday night. Jack and Luke were walking home from football. They walked down a dark alleyway. They had a feeling someone was following them. They started running. Jack tripped over a tree trunk. *Bang!* He banged his head so hard, a trickle of blood left …

Rueben Bernard (10)

St Mary's RC Primary School, Isleworth

I Hate The Dentist

'Come Lisa, we need to go and get your filling
done,' said Mum.
Lisa painted her whole tooth white. 'I don't need
a filling, look!' said Lisa.
'I'm sure that's just food. Here, take it off with
mouthwash,' said Mum.
All the paint came out of her mouth. Oh no!

Ana De Las Cuevas Takahashi (11)
St Mary's RC Primary School, Isleworth

Tiny Treasures Fiction From Middlesex

Dead!

It was 4.15 when Lily returned home and went to her room to study. Suddenly, she heard something downstairs. She went to check it out. She went to the living room and saw a masked man - he had a knife. He took the knife - blood appeared. She was dead!

Natalia Janik (10)
St Mary's RC Primary School, Isleworth

299

The Child-Eating Zombie

'Jack!' shouted Tim. 'Watch out!'
The mansion door collapsed. The noise startled them. A mutated zombie jumped out and attacked. Running, Jack looked back. Tim's legs were being dragged into darkness. His screams were short. Jack knew to stay alive he had to keep moving. The zombie was really close …

Joe Murray (10)
St Mary's RC Primary School, Isleworth

Race

Honk! The race starts - I make sure I start in the right gear. *Zoom!* My competition go past me - but I also maintain my pace. *Crash!* Major collision at front - now's my chance to overtake. *Whoosh!* The final sprint - twenty-five metres to go. *Honk!* Finish. Third - a heroic bronze.

Marc Tidon (11)
St Mary's RC Primary School, Isleworth

One Missed Call

My phone rang. I didn't answer. I saw this girl
following me. Sweat dripped from my forehead.
I turned, I saw my best friend shouting, Run,
Jackie!' I did. My friend got shot. I called 999.
Someone called me again. I answered. A voice
said, 'I'm coming … '

Sean Estavillo
St Mary's RC Primary School, Isleworth

302

Funfair

Three best friends go to the funfair. They decide to go on the ghost train. Really excited, they get on and it drives into the tunnel. Suddenly, it stops and they hear strange noises and feel hands on their shoulders. They run away. They scream, but the doors are locked …

Ciara Foord (11), Athena Elia & Ella Walton (10)
St Mary's RC Primary School, Isleworth

Betrayal

In the dead of night, Jack and Fred break into a
mansion full of valuables. Tragically, Fred is injured
and left behind by his cowardly partner.
Under extreme questioning, Fred gives the police
Jack's name and a deal is struck. Jack is sentenced
to life while Fred happily walks free.

**Callum Ferguson (11), Josh O'Shea &
John Mensah (10)**

St Mary's RC Primary School, Isleworth

Killer Tarantula

Splash! Carrie stepped into a puddle as she read that a tarantula had escaped the zoo. She stood, petrified, feeling four pairs of legs creeping down her neck. *Thump!* She fell dead on the floor - the only evidence that was left was a trickle of blood streaming down her cheek ...

**Adam Lenkiewicz, Marc Tidon (11)
& Rueben Bernard (10)**
St Mary's RC Primary School, Isleworth

Untitled

Grace walked along the deserted beach; she
heard something strange and tried to follow the
sound. Coming to an isolated cave, filled with
curiosity she went inside. Suddenly, a huge stone
rolled over the exit and she was trapped.
'Help! Help!' Her screams echoed ...
It was just a dream. Phew!

**Imogen Wilby, Hannah Wright (11)
& Shechem Tesfaye**
St Mary's RC Primary School, Isleworth

Is It Really Him?

Bang! Oh no! What was that? Quietly, I tiptoed down the corridor. 'I can't believe it, it's Santa, I know it is!'
Feeling both excited and worried, I rolled down the stairs, then, breathless with excitement, I ran to the living room and …
'Oh, it's only Toby!' (Our dog.)

**Jodie Geere, Amy Blewitt
& Charlotte Doyle (10)**
St Mary's RC Primary School, Isleworth

The Wild Ride

'I bagsy the wild ride roller coaster first!'
screamed Holly, running ahead.
'Fasten your seatbelts,' said the attendant.
'Argh, we're at the top!' screamed Lisa.
Suddenly, the ride stopped. Creaking, it gained
speed and seemed to be out of control …
Screaming, smashing, blood, guts … their lives
came to an end.

**Jennifer Samia, Ana De Las Cuevas Takahashi (11)
& Anndior Amoah (10)**
St Mary's RC Primary School, Isleworth

Monkey Mission - The Robbery

Bang! Ninja Monkey smashes through the ceiling
of the bank, winds through the lasers to reach
the vault. Once there, he brings out his banana
gadget, cuts through the vault, takes £1 billion,
calls his helicopter to take him and the money
away to start Monkey FC and dominate world
football!

**Joe Murray, Kyle Junkere
& Tom O'Halloran (11)**
St Mary's RC Primary School, Isleworth

Night In The Museum

'Did he lock us in?'
'Where has everyone gone?'
The children held each other in the darkness.
The light turned on and they found themselves
surrounded by dinosaurs. Dead, battered and
bruised, the children's bodies were stuck in
history.
A search was made, but no one noticed the new
exhibits.

**Anne Omotola, Katrina Nevin
& Sean Estavillo**
St Mary's RC Primary School, Isleworth

Should Have Gone To School

It's 10.30am, should be maths, but Izzy is
shopping instead. Someone grabs her bag.
Terrified, she turns around. There is a masked
man before her.
'Help!'
He lifts his arm and punches her on the nose.
'Where am I?' she asks, sitting in a hospital bed
feeling bruised all over.

**Maria Gabriel (11), Malika Chohan
& Natalia Janik (10)**
St Mary's RC Primary School, Isleworth

Information

We hope you have enjoyed reading this book - and that you will continue to enjoy it in the coming years.

If you like reading and writing, drop us a line or give us a call and we'll send you a free information pack. Alternatively visit our website at www.youngwriters.co.uk

Write to:
Young Writers Information,
Remus House,
Coltsfoot Drive,
Peterborough,
PE2 9JX

Tel: (01733) 890066
Email: youngwriters@forwardpress.co.uk